Dog Can Hop

by Lada Kratky
Illustrations by Doreen Gay-Kassel

HAMPTON-BROWN

Hampton-Brown
P.O. Box 223220
Carmel, CA 93922
1-800-333-3510

Printed in the U.S.A.
ISBN 07362-0541-1
          03 04 05 06 07 08 10 9 8 7 6 5 4

Dog gets a can.

Dog gets a pan.

Dog taps and taps.

Dog wags and wags.

Dog hops and bops!

My Take-Home Book: Short o
BOOK 12

Dog

HAMPTON-BROWN

800-333-3510

9 780736 205412

ISBN 0-7362-0541-1